DISNEP Junior

Fancy NANCY

Nancy Takes the Case

Adapted by Victoria Saxon
Based on the episode
by Laurie Israel

Illustrations by the
Disney Storybook
Art Team

D1451017

HARPER
An Imprint of HarperCollinsPublishers

Sacrebleu! Oh no!

There is a lot of snow outside.

My friends and I have been

stuck playing inside for hours.

Lionel is reading a comic out loud
to Bok Bok, his toy chicken.

Wanda and Rhonda are playing
with a balloon.
They start to fight.

Grace is looking at a catalog.

She wants to pick out

some gifts for herself.

Grace and Lionel start to fight.

"Lionel, shh," says Grace.

"I like hearing Lionel's
comic books," says Bree.

JoJo and Frenchy escape.

"Come on, Frenchy," JoJo says.

"Everyone, *arretez*!" I say.

That's French for stop.

"I know we have been stuck

in this house forever,

but we can still have fun."

I try to get my friends to play

Who Could Have Done It?

It's my favorite board game.

But they do not want to play.

They want to go home.

"Wait a minute," Lionel says.

"One of my comic books is missing."

"A missing comic book

can only mean one thing," I say.

"Someone stole it!"

Ooh la la! It's a real life mystery to solve.

"We must investigate," I say. That's fancy for study the facts to decide who could have done it.

I'm practically an expert
at detective work.
"It's time we get serious
about this case," I tell Bree.
"Let's go pick out our outfits."

When we return, we ask our friends
where they last saw the comic book.

I question everyone.

Bree sketches the crime scene.

At last we finish.

We look at Bree's drawing.

"Everyone had the chance
to take it," Lionel says.

Next I look at motives.

That's fancy for

why someone would do something.

I talk to Rhonda first.

"Why did you take the

comic?" I ask.

"I didn't," says Rhonda.

Then I question Wanda.

I look her in the eye.

"Bet you I can keep from blinking

longer than you," she says.

"Did you steal the comic book
to keep Lionel from reading
too loud?" I ask Grace.

Grace rolls her eyes.

"Puh-lease," she says.

I even ask Lionel if he took
his own comic book as a joke.
Lionel holds up Bok Bok.
"No!" he says, in his best
chicken voice.

"You don't really believe *I* did it,"

Bree says when I ask her.

"I'm a detective, Bree," I say.

"I believe nothing . . . and everything."

23

"You like comics too," Bree says.

Everyone in the room looks at me.

They think I took the comic book!

"I couldn't have stolen it," I say,

"but I know who did!"

I pick up an envelope.

"The answer is in here," I say.

I put the envelope in the kitchen.

Then I leave the room.

It's a trap.

I am sure the thief will take it!

When I return,
everyone is in the kitchen.
Nobody took the envelope.
"Tell us who did it,"
my friends say.

Before I tell them I don't know,
we hear a noise in the living room.
It must be the thief!

It's JoJo!

She has the comic book.

"I like the pictures," she says.

JoJo hands me the comic book.

"I believe this belongs to you,"
I say, handing the comic to Lionel.
"*Voilà!* This case is closed!"

Fancy Nancy's Fancy Words

These are the fancy words in this book:

Sacrebleu—French for oh no

Arretez—French for stop

Ooh la la—French for wow

Investigate—study the facts to decide
who could have done it

Motive—why someone would do
something

Voilà—French for look at that